S.R. Martin

INSOMNIACS

ROAD KILL

SCHOLASTIC INC.
New York Toronto London Auckland Sydney
Mexico City New Delhi Hong Kong

ISBN 0-590-69130-9

12 11 10 9 8 7 6 5 4 3 2 1   9/9 0 1 2 3 4/0

Printed in the U.S.A.

First Scholastic printing, March 1999

CHAPTER ONE

The accident happened about fifty miles east of Madura, on the Nullarbor Plain.

I was with my parents and twin sisters on the way back to Adelaide from an extended fishing trip in Esperance at the tail end of our Christmas vacation. We'd spent the preceding three weeks living in a tent at the campground there, rising early with my father to launch the old rowboat onto the dead-calm waters of the Southern Ocean. Dad and I would trail thin handlines behind the boat for queen snapper and boar fish, sharing crackers and cheese washed down with a thermos of hot, sweet tea for breakfast.

We'd also share long periods of silence and occasional meandering conversations about Mom and the twins, how school was going, what I wanted to be when I grew up, and what life was like for Dad when he was my age. I'd never understood just how different things must have been for him, in a world without personal computers, where television was a luxury even for rich people, and where people actually listened to what was being said on the radio.

It was a peaceful time, and one where I realized that Dad and I really hadn't had all that much time to talk over the previous year. He'd be off to work before I woke up in the mornings, and when he came home at night he'd be too tired to talk much and I'd be off in my room with my homework. Weekends he spent keeping our rambling garden in check.

Dad and I weren't the best fishermen in the world (as Mom would often say when we came back empty-handed around lunchtime), but we weren't the worst, either; and I'd made my father enormously proud when I landed an especially large snapper — cutting two fingers on my left hand with the line in the process. It was on the day before our vacation in Esperance ended, and we'd brought it back to shore, took photos of the two of us holding the fish with its startling blue fluorescent marking down its back, then filleted it and fried it in a huge pan that night for dinner. There was so much fish left over, we gave the remaining pieces to the people in the next tent, who were probably a lot worse at fishing than Dad and me.

It was a great evening, the five of us sitting around our little gas camp stove outside the tent, the smell and sizzle of frying fish filling the air combined with the sound of trees sighing at each other in the evening breeze. You could hear the laughter and conversations of the other campers, the sound of boats being launched for bouts of evening fishing, the occasional rising buzz of a mosquito passing your ear. My mother was rolling around in the sand with my sisters, wrestling and giggling as they tried to tickle one another senseless, while my father covered the fillets in flour and dropped them into the crackle and steam of the frying pan. I sat in one of our camp chairs, half listening to a tape that was running a little slow because the batteries in the tape deck were about to die. As my father finished each golden fillet, he'd pass it across to me and I'd drain off the excess butter with a paper towel.

We ate them with salad and a giant loaf of crusty bread that my mother had bought from the town bakery that afternoon, breaking chunks of it off in our hands and using it to wipe up the remaining salad oils and fragments from our tin plates.

I don't think I'd eaten a better meal in my entire life (not that, at my age, I'd had an especially long one), and I think it had a lot to do with the fact that I had been responsible for providing the fish. Somehow, when you go out and catch something yourself, it just seems to taste better. Don't ask me why, it just does.

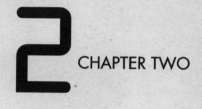

CHAPTER TWO

The next morning we packed up our tent and gear, attached the boat trailer to the back of our old station wagon, piled my still sleepy sisters into the back, and drove off into the sunrise.

And drove and drove and drove. Until, when we passed through Madura, the sun had fallen behind us and we were surrounded by the eerie twilight of the Nullarbor, the longest and flattest piece of country in the world.

Mom and Dad talked briefly about stopping when we got gas at Madura, but Dad being Dad figured we could go "just a bit further, to the next town at least" before we checked into a motel for the night. Everyone was wide-awake and we'd been singing rounds in the car for the last hundred or so miles, so there wasn't a lot of disagreement.

We went barreling off into the night, the station wagon's headlights seeming to create their own bright yellow tunnel through the rapidly thickening darkness. My sisters were singing "Frère Jacques," which they'd just learned before school had let out for vacation, and Dad was trying to do harmonies in his dreadfully off-key voice, when I dropped something onto the floor of the car. It's weird now, because I remember everything that happened in such crystal-clear detail, but I can't for the life of me remember what it was that I dropped. All I know is that I did something really dumb, something that I'd never done before. I undid my seat belt and leaned down to pick it up.

My father was half looking back over his shoulder, singing along with the girls, when I heard my mother shout, "Look out!" and I heard my father swear violently, which is something he only does on special occasions.

And then everything turned into chaos.

It probably only took a few seconds, but seemed to go on for eternity.

I remember looking up when I heard my mother shout and seeing this huge kangaroo that appeared to be flying toward the front of the car. That, I think, was an optical illusion caused by the speed of the car and the kangaroo crossing in front of it, but for a moment there I had the distinct impression that this massive creature had flown down out of the night and was swooping toward the windshield of our car.

Then it hit.

My father didn't even have time to hit the brakes, just careened straight into it, and the noise of it thumping across the hood and erupting through the windshield were the loudest sounds I think I've ever heard. I remember wondering at the time how something that had seemed to be floating toward us could hit with such force, but I never got to resolve that in my mind.

From then on it was a complete catastrophe, with glass and screams and everything swirling around like images from a kaleidoscope.

And then I was flying. What happened when my father's foot eventually found the brake was that I went straight out through the hole the kangaroo came in through, sailing out of the noise and drama inside the car into a strange, dark place inhabited only by the whistle of the passing air. I must have been twisting about in the air because at one stage I remember seeing our car flipping over and rolling, its lights spinning crazily, and this little voice in my head saying, "I hope they're all right, I hope they're all right."

Which, as it happens, they were. As all right as you can be, anyway, when an extremely large, bounding marsupial comes crashing through your front windshield when you're doing around sixty-five miles an hour, causing your car to flip over and roll along a highway in the middle of nowhere. They were all unconscious when a truck stopped an hour later and managed to summon help on a CB radio. Apart from cuts and bruises (Dad had the imprint of a kangaroo paw on the side of his face for months) and an enormous amount of confusion about what happened, they were fine. It was the seat belts that saved them, and my lack of one that caused my flight.

But that's their story, not mine. What happened to me was quite different.

CHAPTER THREE

What happened to me was downright strange.

So I'm flying, right?

I've seen the car roll and then passed on from that, and I'm in this sort of half-state, not quite sure what's happening, if I'm alive or dead or what. I mean, I'd heard stories about people rising above stuff when they were dying, seeing themselves on an operating table or their loved ones trying to perform mouth-to-mouth while they're floating up above and watching it all. Then all of a sudden they're sucked back down and into their bodies and they wake up and talk about it and everyone thinks they're crazy.

Well, I wasn't crazy. And I wasn't dying, either. I was just flying through the air.

I worked that out when I landed.

WHUMP!

I'm not sure if it was the noise of me hitting the earth or the sound of all the air in my body leaving in such a hurry. But it was loud.

There was a soft sand underneath me; I could feel that quite clearly, because my hands were clutching at it, as if by holding onto something I could get some of the air back into my lungs.

It didn't work. The more I tried to suck in air, the less my lungs seemed to want it. I must have looked like some gigantic goldfish that's suddenly flipped itself straight out of its tank, madly trying to suck in something that its body simply isn't designed to handle.

The last thing I remember is the stars, millions and millions of them. They are really quite beautiful out there in the middle of nowhere. I lay there looking up at them, thinking that maybe I should give them a quick count before I died. But then they started spinning, and that just made me feel sick.

They spun and spun, coming closer and closer together, until they all joined up as one tiny pinprick of light.

The light blinked out.

My first sensation after that — and I really have no idea how long after it was — was of a gentle hand patting my cheek.

It was a nice sensation and made me feel peaceful, like something Mom might have done if I was sick in bed at home. I really didn't want to open my eyes, just lie there feeling the gentle touch of fingers.

For a while I wondered if the accident had been a dream, but I could still feel the same soft sand under my fingers and smell the dry desert air, and there was a terrible dull throb which was coming from my back and seemed to spread out to inhabit every inch of my body.

Pain equaled accident, so I knew it wasn't a dream.

I knew I'd been found because I could hear the dull murmur of voices, but I couldn't quite hear what they were saying.

I'm safe, I was thinking, safe and sound and about to be on my way home.

"I think we should eat him," I heard a voice say quite close to my ear, and that made me open my eyes very, very quickly.

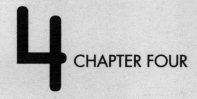

CHAPTER FOUR

Now, I've never been much of a reader of books, but I've sure seen a lot of movies and I've played an awful lot of video games, so when I say the face that was looking down at me was hideous, I know what I'm talking about.

The demons out of Mortal Kombat had nothing on this guy (if he even was a guy — it was hard to be certain of anything about these creatures).

Its face was sort of melted — I guess that's the best way to describe it—and though it had all the usual features you'd associate with a person, like a nose and two eyes, ears, and a mouth, they all seemed to blur and meld together with its skin, which was all warty and had dried flakes all over it, a tiny bit like scales. There was hair as well, though not a great deal of it, and what there was wasn't confined to its head. In fact, the greatest amount of it protruded from its nose and ears in strange little tufts, the hairs themselves being long, black, and extremely wiry.

It grinned down at me, exposing a row of jagged, yellowing teeth all caked together with so much plaque it was difficult to tell which was which.

"Hey, it's not dead. It just opened its eyes," it said with a gust of breath that would have gagged a sewer rat.

I moaned and tried to roll sideways, though I'm not sure if I was trying to escape its face or its breath, and the wave of pain that hit me almost made me pass out again.

"We can't eat it if it's still alive," I heard it continue.

Then several voices joined in what sounded like a chant. "If it ain't kill, it ain't to be killed."

There was a hurried scuttling and I felt my shoulder grabbed by a large, clawed hand which rolled me over onto my back again. A second melted face joined the first, blinking angrily down at me with red-rimmed eyes.

"Then we'll wait," it said, and I could hear definite satisfaction in its voice. "From the look of it, we won't be sitting around for long."

It poked me with one of its clawed fingers.

"Nice fat little fella, too. He'll taste real nice."

That was it for me.

"I'm not fat," I croaked at it, and was delighted to see that both creatures jumped back, registering surprise. "I'm generously muscled!"

"If it talks, it walks," came another chorus of voices.

"That's not talking," the second creature shouted over its shoulder, "that's croaking, and if we can eat frogs, we can eat it."

The first creature moved over to look down at me again. "We only eat frogs that have stopped croaking, as you very well know, Crik, so the point is moot. It said it wasn't fat."

"So it lies. And anyway, it only sort of speaks like us. What on earth does being 'gebrously mumbled' mean?" the one called Crik sneered.

I was indignantly about to correct the creature's pronunciation when I heard the sounds of cars stopping not too far away, the slamming of doors, and voices shouting. The nicest thing about it was, they were shouting my name.

Opening my mouth, I was about to let out the yell of my life when one of the clawed hands slammed down and covered the lower half of my face, turning my yell into a series of muffled grunts. Among the voices calling, I was sure I could hear my father, which caused me to begin struggling violently. All this resulted in was a couple more clawed hands pinning me securely to the ground and the one called Crik leaning close to my ear and whispering, "If you shout, my little fat friend, I'll rip your face off and eat it in front of you."

That shut me up very effectively.

"They're coming," the first creature whispered. "We're going to have to leave him."

"We can't leave him, idiot," Crik hissed

back. "He's seen us. No one's allowed to see us. You know the rules."

"You weren't so worried about the rules a minute ago."

Then I heard the chorus of voices again, though this time in a low murmur, like the sound of wind moaning through trees late at night.

"We are the eyes in the night; we don't exist in the light."

"See," Crik hissed. "Everyone agrees."

There was a pause while the other considered.

"Bring him, then," he said.

A hand gripped me by the hair and I suddenly took off backward as if I were on some supersonic ride at an amusement park.

I guess it was dawn, because I could see things fairly well, in a strange, tossed-about way. It's hard to see or think anything clearly when you're being dragged along on your back through rough undergrowth by a pack of nightmarish creatures who sometimes ran on two legs, and at other times on all fours. And I wasn't conscious all the time, that's for sure. I would be for a while, and I'd see this crazed vision of sky and bushes and hideous faces and bodies, then I'd pass out again. Physically, I was aware of the pain of being dragged along by my hair, and of rocks and sticks and things stabbing into my back. There was the sound of the creatures' feet slapping hugely against the ground and their harsh, wheezing breathing all around me.

There were periods, though — I have no idea of how long — when I'd be in this blissful floating state, as if I were held up by clouds, and I'd see things from different times in my life: the trip to Esperance, times at school, playing with my sisters, being thrown in the air by my mother (that must have been a while back, because my mother hasn't been able to lift me for years), playing with friends in the backyard of our home in Henley Beach. Everything was jumbled together, but in a nice way, sort of like a bag of mixed lollipops with all your favorite flavors.

I didn't mind being like that. It was being jerked back to the bizarre drag race along the desert floor that I didn't like.

Then we went down the hole, and I lost it completely.

5 CHAPTER FIVE

Up until that time I'd had a certain amount of control over my behavior. Sure, everything was strange, but I hadn't gone ballistic, which you'd think would be a normal reaction. Truth is, I think I was in shock most of the time, but I came out of it really fast when I realized what was happening.

You see, I'm claustrophobic.

Really claustrophobic.

I even get panicky in the toilet stalls at

school, which occasionally leads to extreme bouts of constipation. But that's another story.

Anyway, how far we traveled from the site of the accident I have no idea, but all of a sudden I snapped out of my blissful floating state to realize that we were starting to head downward. I could still see the sky, but was aware of the earth closing in on both sides.

Then the sky went as well.

I was quiet for a couple of seconds, unsure of exactly what was happening, then I felt my skin start to prickle the way it does when I'm in a too-confined space, and the sweat started to rise up out of my skin, and those little flashing lights started behind my eyes, and my muscles started twitching all by themselves, and the beast inside me came rushing out.

I really am the walking definition of fury when this happens. In fact, fury really doesn't describe it, because it goes beyond that. There really is someone else inside me at these times, and I have no control over who he is.

I know what he's doing, but I have as much chance of controlling what he does as I have of becoming the Pope.

Zilch!

Seemingly without any instruction from me, my hands rose up behind my head, found the hairy buttocks of the creature that was dragging me, and dug their fingers in as deep as they could go. This brought a very definite howl of pain (and way back inside where the real me was still residing, I had a certain satisfaction in recognizing the howl as belonging to Crik), and all of a sudden my hair was released. Now normally, this should have caused me a great deal of satisfaction, as being dragged along by your hair (which was rather long, straggly, and blond) is extremely unpleasant, but I was in no mood for being satisfied. My arms and legs were going haywire, kicking and punching in all directions. There was a low, ugly growl coming from my throat, and I could feel my teeth clenched so tightly I'm amazed they didn't explode with the pressure.

The beast was out and he wasn't going anywhere quietly, especially if it involved going underground.

For a moment there it seemed as if I were on top of everything. We were in a low earth tunnel, which I was able to crouch in, and back the way we'd just come from I could still see the gray-blue of the sky. Between myself and the sky, however, there were three or four of the creatures, but they didn't look like they'd be a problem getting past, as they were cowering as far away from my furious self as they could.

(To be honest, I'd have been cowering, too, if someone were making the sort of noises I could hear coming from my throat.)

I bared my teeth, gave out a massive howl of rage and triumph, and was about to make one almighty rush toward the light, away from the claustrophobic tunnel that had turned me into a madman, when I heard a voice that was almost as angry as mine coming from the tunnel behind me.

"Now you've really done it, fat boy!"

Furious, I turned back to confront it.

I caught one quick glimpse of Crik's snarling face, and that's the very last thing I remember about the tunnel.

CHAPTER SIX

Firelight.

It was flickering across a high ceiling, sometimes like a dance of orange light, other times a soft, slow undulation of color.

I was on my back again, but this time I was tied.

Slowly, I began to turn my head. Not a great deal, because moving it really hurt, and I seemed to have developed an extra nose between my eyes, which throbbed continually.

I was in a very large cave. So large, in fact, that I wasn't feeling at all claustrophobic. At least, not immediately, anyway.

The roof against which the firelight was playing was at least seven feet high, if not higher, and was no more threatening than the ceiling of a house. Glancing to the side, I could see the walls, but they were far enough away that I didn't even break out in a sweat.

A fire was burning quite close by and there was a figure tending it. At least I presumed that's what it was there to do, because it wasn't moving when I looked at it. It was just sort of hunched over between me and the fire, with its back to me. Apart from what looked like a huge pile of rugs over in one corner, the cave was basically empty.

I tried gently twisting my hands, but it

44

didn't do any good. It felt like they were bound in iron, even though there was a certain amount of give in it and my fingers weren't numb, which meant there was circulation in them.

"You're wasting your time wriggling," came a low, rather gentle voice. "I don't think anything could break kangaroo sinew."

The figure at the fire shifted slightly, so I guessed that was who was talking.

Now that it knew I was awake there was no point being subtle, so I lifted my hands and had a look at the bonds. They seemed to be made from white plastic, and though there was some give, they were still incredibly strong.

"What did you just say?" I asked.

"Kangaroo sinew," the voice replied. "You're tied with kangaroo sinew. It's very strong. We use it for lots of things."

By wriggling, hunching my back, and pushing with my feet (which were also bound in the same material) I managed to get myself into a sitting position and have more of a look around.

The floor of the cave was strewn with white bones of all shapes and sizes, some of which were too big to have even come from a person, and there was the pervasive smell of something that reminded me of bad meat. Scattered about were various animal skins, and there were skulls of kangaroos, cattle, and dingoes sitting in little nooks cut into the cave walls. What I had originally thought was a large pile of rugs in one corner turned out to be a group of the creatures. They were all jumbled together, sleeping in a great huddle of bodies, snoring and snorting and twitching away without a care in the world. The light from the fire illuminated strange paintings on the cave walls, and after staring at them for a while I realized what they were. Pictures of cars. Hundreds of them. And they weren't just the everyday cars I was familiar with, but older ones as well, including those humpbacked things called VW Bugs that my father used to get all misty-eyed about.

All the pictures showed pretty much the same thing — cars running over animals.

The creature at the fire had now turned around and was watching me inspect the cave walls with an expression I could only describe as pure curiosity. It would look at my face, then turn to see what I was looking at, then quickly look back at me again to see my reaction to the picture. Eventually it spoke.

"You like Art?"

"Pardon?"

"Our Art. You seem to be interested in our Art."

"Is that what it is?"

It shuffled closer to me and I could see that it was extremely old, much older than Crik and the others that had brought me to the cave. Wrinkles covered not just its face but its whole body, and the hairs that protruded from its nose and ears were pure white. The eyes were watery and one had what looked like a milky film stretched across it. When I talked I could see that its teeth were worn down to yellow stumps, which looked like the foundations of some lost city sticking up from its brown gums.

"Are you being rude?" it asked, with a definite sense of curiosity in its voice.

"No. I'm being extremely pissed off, which I think I have every right to be. Wouldn't you be if you'd been thrown from a car, kidnapped by some nightmare with bad breath, dragged through a desert, pulled down a hole, punched in the nose, and then tied up with animal scraps?" I could hear my voice getting louder and louder as I listed the crimes against me, and I resolved to try and remain more in control until I knew more about what was happening.

The creature, however, just cocked its head to one side and listened patiently. In fact, I'm sure I saw it smile.

"You haven't been kidnapped," it replied. "You were given to us."

"Given to you? How could I be given to you?"

"You were a gift from The Travelers of The Black Track, the ones with the fearsome eyes who roar and fling aside all who cross their path. They provide us with everything. They give us The Kill."

It looked hard at me to gauge my reaction.

I looked back at the pictures on the wall.

"The Travelers of The Black Track? You mean cars, don't you?" I asked.

"Cars?"

"Yeah, cars. You know. With the fearsome eyes and all that stuff. They're cars. That's what I came out of. I was in a car accident."

The creature shook its head. "You were a gift. There was nothing accidental about it. Everything that lies alongside The Black Track is a gift from The Travelers. I've been waiting a long time for you."

"You have?"

"Only once before have they given one of their own. Many, many years ago, in the time of my grandparents. He taught us The Speech and The Fire, and told us that one day we would come out from the dark and travel The Black Track like The Gods. Unfortunately he was very sick and eventually he died." It cocked its head again. "You are a God, aren't you?"

I lifted my bound hands and waved them in front of its face.

"If I'm a God, what am I doing tied up?"

"You were angry, and you nearly tore off Crik's backside."

"He wanted to eat me! He'd just dragged me along by my hair! He was taking me down a hole in the ground! Of course I was angry."

"He still wants to eat you," the creature said.

I swallowed loudly. "He does?"

"Crik doesn't think you're a God. He says you're too small and weak."

"We come in all shapes and sizes. There are smaller ones than me. My sisters, for instance. They're tiny. You're not going to let him eat me, are you?"

I started to shiver and looked across at the pile of sleeping creatures to see if I could recognize Crik, but they were too jumbled up to make head or tail out of anything.

The old creature scratched its head with a long, cracked claw.

"Well, to be quite honest, he can't actually eat you. If it ain't kill, it ain't to be killed," he said, and I recognized the line that I'd heard chanted when I was lying back by the accident site.

"That's very reassuring," I muttered.

"Crik and Strang have been arguing about what to do with you ever since they brought you back to the cave. They share the decision making, so they have to agree before anything can happen. And that's not often, because they're so different."

Strang, I gathered, was the other creature who'd been talking with Crik when they found me, the one I'd first seen when I woke up. He wasn't exactly pretty, but I hoped he was on my side.

"What about you?" I asked. "Aren't you in charge? You seem to be the oldest."

"I," he said proudly, "am the keeper of The History and The Fire. I take no part in the making of decisions. But yes, I am the oldest."

"So it's up to Bib and Bub, then, is it?"

"Pardon?"

"Crock and String."

"Excuse me?"

"Nothing." I sulked.

The creature looked at me strangely, then turned back to the fire. He poked his long claws into the embers and stirred them around, bringing out what looked like a charred branch. He wiped the ashes off and I was suddenly overwhelmed by the most delicious odor. My stomach started to rumble loudly and I wondered how long it had been since I'd eaten. We hadn't stopped for dinner yet when the accident happened, and I'd been unconscious at least a couple of times since then, so it had to have been quite a few hours, if not days.

The sound of my stomach stopped the creature in midbite. It looked across at me and pointed the charred stick in my direction.

"You sound hungry. Do you want something to eat?"

I looked at the black thing in front of my face. It didn't look at all appealing, but it smelled sensational. In the end I had no choice in the matter, because my stomach let loose a growl that could have come from a rabid dog and my mouth sprang open of its own accord.

My teeth cut through charcoal and my mouth was filled with the delicious taste of grilled meat. I tore off a huge chunk of it, chewed madly, and I could feel the juices running down my chin.

"My, my," said the creature, "we are hungry, aren't we?"

"Narving," I said around the mouthful of food. "Now nong nave I neen 'ere?"

It looked at me quizzically. I swallowed.

"How long have I been here?" I said, stretching my head out toward the food.

"About a day. Crik brought you in as the sun was coming up, and it'll be going down again soon. That's when everyone will wake up and we can get on with the test."

"What test?" I said as I tore off another chunk of mystery meat. "And just what am I eating?"

"The test to see if you're a God," it said, taking a small bite itself. "And you're eating fresh kangaroo. Only a day or two old, I'd say. Hardly any maggots in it at all."

CHAPTER SEVEN

After I'd finished throwing up, I fell into a hazy kind of sleep for a while — the result of tiredness, pain, sensory overload, and having just emptied my stomach of half-rotten road kill. I didn't dream of anything, but I was aware of noises around me, occasional voices, and the continued smell of cooking kangaroo.

When I opened my eyes everyone was awake. Crik and Strang were sitting with the old creature near the fire. They were mumbling amongst themselves and looking across in my direction. Other creatures were moving around in the cave, some eating, others giving themselves a good licking, like cats do when they're cleaning themselves.

By this time they'd started to remind me of something, but I couldn't quite put my finger on what it was. It was as if they were a cross between people and something large, heavyset, and hairy. The answer was flitting around in the deeper shadows of my brain, occasionally showing glimpses of itself, then disappearing into the darkness again.

Then the old creature clapped its hands and everyone in the cave formed a circle around the fire, which basically left me as the center of attention. They bowed their heads and the old one started to recite in a loud, singsong voice.

"This is The History. First there was The

Bang, and it shook the earth asunder, destroying everything in its path. It caved in the burrows and the dust rose in a great cloud that covered the sky, and the earth below turned to glass. From below the glass came The Mother and The Father, and in great fear they fled their home and traveled for many days and nights without food or water. They were lost and frightened and their skin was burned black. One night they came upon The Black Track, where The Travelers with fearsome eyes came roaring and thundering past, and they would not cross it. It brought a great fear to them, and they cowered alongside it, because they could not go back and they could not go forward. They thought they would die."

"They thought they would die," the others chanted.

"But they did not die," the old one continued. "When the dawn came The Travelers had left a gift alongside The Black Track. It was The Gift of blood and hair and meat, and though The Mother and The Father had never touched Kill before, their hunger was so great that they accepted The Gift, and The Gift gave them life."

"The Gift gave them life."

"And so they lived alongside The Black Track and bore children, and the children bore children, and each generation accepted The Gift from The Travelers, and we grew stronger and changed. And with each generation the changes were better for us, until we rose upon our two legs and ran. And then The Traveler came upon us and he was very sick and he talked in prophecy, which the children learned. We gave him Kill and he gave us The Fire and The Speech and The Three Laws. Then he, too, died, and he gave us himself."

"He gave us himself."

At this stage in The History, as they called it, I started to become very nervous. I wanted to ask just what they meant by "He gave us himself," but I thought it would be rude to interrupt.

Then they all started chanting together.

"If it ain't kill, it ain't to be killed.

"If it talks, it walks.

"We are the eyes in the night; we don't exist in the light."

I reckoned whoever this guy was, he wasn't talking in prophecy. He was delirious, but I could understand the confusion.

There was a period of silence as they all stood there with their eyes closed and their heads down. Then my old friend Crik suddenly snapped his head up, looked directly at me, and snarled, "Okay, let's take fat boy out and see if he's a God."

I swallowed very loudly.

CHAPTER EIGHT

They untied my legs, which was something, but then they made me go out through the tunnel.

"You try throwing a fit again," Crik whispered in my ear, "and I'll chew off every bit of you that gets out of line."

He meant it, too, and the fear of Crik kept my claustrophobia almost in check. Oh, I sweated and trembled and I could feel the beast raging to get out, but I really didn't think he'd have much of a chance against Crik this time, especially since the element of surprise would be missing. After what seemed like hours, I was suddenly out in the open again.

I gave out a loud whoop of success, my delight at having passed through a closed space without turning crazy overcoming my general fear of the situation.

Crik gave me a clap over the head, but even that didn't bother me. I'd conquered my fear for the first time, and it made me elated.

Then they made me run.

There was a full moon out over the desert and it lit up the gray bush and tufts of grass. The air was crystal clear and it ripped into my lungs, clearing out the smell of rotting meat, unwashed bodies, and grilling kanga-roo.

The carpet of stars glittered brilliantly, and though my hands were tied and I was being forced to trot along with a small herd of hairy mutants, I was overwhelmed by the beauty of it all, and I felt like leaping up to try and touch it, to glide into it and become a tiny glittering body floating above the earth forever.

We came up over a small rise in the earth and there before me was Highway One. It was defined by the lights of cars and trucks and seemed to stretch in both directions as far as the eyes could see.

"The Black Track," said Crik reverentially.

"Highway One," I replied. "That's what The Travelers call it, Crik."

He gave me such a wallop across the head, I rolled down the rise in the earth for quite some distance before coming to rest with my face rammed tight in a bush. I was hauled back to my feet.

"We'll see how smart you are in just a few minutes, fat boy, when we test you out on The Track."

"What are you going to do?" I squeaked, afraid now that I'd been shown just how weak I was compared to Crik.

"You'll see." He smiled at me.

We were at the road before I knew it, crouched down amongst the bushes that grew close alongside the asphalt. The heat from the day was still radiating out from it, and I could smell exhaust fumes and rubber faintly in the air. Every now and then a car would hurtle past, making the air swirl around us. Cars traveled very fast out here and I was suddenly very nervous about what Crik had in mind.

He turned to me. "We're going to test you with one of the really big ones. If you live, I'll accept you as a God. If you don't, you'll become Kill and I'll have you for breakfast. Fair enough?"

"Are you going to untie my hands?"

"Gods don't need their hands." Crik grinned.

I really didn't like the idea of being thrown in front of a truck traveling over sixty-five miles an hour in the middle of the night, but I didn't think I was going to get much choice in the matter.

"Here comes one," I heard someone whisper, and suddenly Crik and Strang were holding one of my arms each, crouching by the side of the road.

In the distance I could see the blazing headlights of a massive truck and all the little colored lights the drivers like to put all over the cabin. The closer it got, the bigger it became.

I started to struggle violently, but I was held firm.

"One, two, three," Strang counted.

Then, just as they threw me out onto the highway, I managed to get my arm away from Strang and, though I was still being propelled out onto the road, I lifted both my arms and looped them around Crik's neck.

The two of us tumbled out onto the road.

Crik screamed as if I'd just bitten his nose off.

We rolled and struggled into the middle of the road, Crik biting and scratching and screaming, "No! No! No!" at the top of his lungs.

He struggled so violently, he snapped the bonds around my wrists, and I rolled free, jumped frantically to my feet, and scooted off the opposite side of the road. I collapsed into the bush, looking back over my shoulder in case of pursuit, but Crik was just standing there frozen in the middle of the road, staring at the rapidly approaching truck.

And then I realized something. The others hadn't tried to help him. And I suddenly knew why.

They never came onto the road. The Black Track was sacred, which was also why Crik hadn't run. It was also why he was frozen solid like a rabbit in headlights. He simply didn't know what to do.

He was terrified.

Now, don't ask me why I did it, because I have no real idea. But I suddenly felt sorry for him. He looked so small and frightened and alone. And he was about to be turned into road kill.

Without any direction from my brain, my legs suddenly took off and I ran into him, pushing as hard as I could. He didn't even see me, he was so transfixed by the lights of the approaching truck, which lit the both of us in a brilliant, unearthly glow.

I slammed into him and he disappeared into the darkness on the side of the road. There was a deafening squeal of brakes and the sound of a horn that would have woken people all the way to China, and suddenly I was standing looking directly into a truck grille covered in squashed bugs, enveloped in the smell of hot metal and burning rubber.

I lived, obviously. But only by about an inch.

Weird thing was, the driver knew exactly who I was. They'd been radioing truckers on CBs up and down the highway either side of Madura, telling everyone to keep an eye out for a lost boy.

I've never seen my parents look happier. And my sisters were pretty psyched as well.

I never told anyone what happened. Not

that anyone would believe me if I did. It's just too hard to explain.

One good thing that's come of it, though, is that I seem to be pretty much over my claustrophobia. I have a few nightmares, however, in place of it.

And I've developed an unusually high interest in a place called Maralinga and the nuclear testing that went on there in the fifties.

My teachers think I'm developing an interest in history.

They don't know the half of it.

S.R. MARTIN

S.R. Martin was born and grew up in the beachside suburbs of Perth, Australia. A fascination with the ocean led to an early career in marine biology, but this was cut short when he decided the specimens he collected looked better under an orange-and-cognac sauce than they did under a microscope. After even quicker careers in banking, teaching, and journalism, a wanderlust led him through most of Australia's capital cities and then on to periods of time living in Hong Kong, Taiwan, South Korea, the United Kingdom, and the United States. Returning to Australia, he settled for Melbourne and a career as a freelance writer. In addition to the Insomniacs series, S.R. Martin is the author of *Swampland*, coming soon from Scholastic.